A Horse of a Different Color

Dorothy Hinshaw Patent

A Horse of a Different Color

PHOTOGRAPHS BY William Muñoz

Dodd, Mead & Company · New York

ACKNOWLEDGMENTS

The author and photographer wish to thank all the people who let us take pictures of their horses for this book. Special thanks also go to Donna Hyora, Diane Olson, and Martin Burris for their help.

PHOTOGRAPH CREDITS

The photographs on pages 10 and 29 are by Dorothy Hinshaw Patent. All other photographs are by William Muñoz.

Published by Dodd, Mead & Company, Inc.,
71 Fifth Avenue, New York, N.Y. 10003

Printed in the United States of America by Horowitz/Rae
Designed by Sylvia Frezzolini

1   2   3   4   5   6   7   8   9   10

Library of Congress Cataloging-in-Publication Data
Patent, Dorothy Hinshaw.   A horse of a different color / Dorothy Hinshaw Patent ; photographs by William Muñoz.   p.   cm.   Includes index.   Summary: Introduces the many colors and patterns occurring in horses, including the spotted pinto, dappled, two-tone, solid, and Appaloosa horses.
ISBN 0-396-08836-8
1. Horses—Color—Juvenile literature.   [1. Horses—Color.   2. Horse breeds.]
I. Muñoz, William, ill.   II. Title.
SF279.P38   1988   636.1—dc19   87-25165   CIP   AC

For all the children who love
colorful horses

Contents

Chapter One

The Colorful Horse

Do you have a favorite color for horses? Perhaps you are a fan of the spotted pinto, or maybe your heart beats faster when you see a pure white horse galloping across the pasture or read about the black stallion. Luckily, horses come in a wonderful variety of colors and patterns, enough to please all kinds of horse lovers.

Before people tamed them, horses had only a few colors. Their manes and tails were dark, and their bodies were some shade of tan. But humans like variety, so when they began to keep horses, they often valued animals that looked different. Horses became more and more varied in color, as people often chose to breed animals with unusual colors. Today, scientists trying to understand how horse color is passed on from one generation to the next, or inherited, have difficulty. Since about twenty different units of

The Przewalski horse is the only remaining species of true wild horse.

heredity, or *genes*, affect horse color, it can be hard to predict what color a foal, or baby horse, might be. What breeders hope for, based on the parents, may not be the final result.

Some people like the palomino, with its shiny golden body and flowing white mane and tail. Others want a snow-white mount or a glistening black one. To many, spots or patches of color improve the beauty of the horse. The Arabs, who were among the greatest horse breeders of all time, had very definite opinions about the value of different colors. A coal black horse was admired for its spirit and breathtaking beauty, while they said of a white horse, "In the sun he melts like butter, in the rain he dissolves like salt."

You can't tell what color a baby horse will be by looking at its mother.

Foal Colors

When a foal is born, it may be a different color than what it will grow into. Usually, the foal's coat is lighter than its adult color. The pattern at birth also may be different from the adult. A foal might be born a solid color and develop spots later. Or it could begin with a solid color and shed to a shade of gray when it loses its foal coat. Horse breeders trying to get certain colors may be frustrated when their young horses change color on them.

This Belgian foal will probably grow up to be about the same color as its mother.

What Makes the Colors

It is hard to believe that the many different colors of horses all come from only two similar chemicals, called *pigments*, in the horse's hair. Both are forms of *melanin*, the same pigment that gives human skin its color. When your skin darkens in the summer, it has made more melanin to protect it from the sun's rays. In horses, the melanin may be in the form of *eumelanin*, which is brown or black. Or, it can be present as a reddish pigment called *phaeomelanin*. Both show up as microscopic droplets in the hair. The number of droplets and their arrangement make the coat appear a

The tan hairs on this horse have less melanin than the black ones.

particular color. If a lot of melanin is there in droplets of a particular shape, the horse is black. A small amount of melanin in differently shaped droplets will make the hair tan. Lots of phaeomelanin results in a gleaming, deep red coat, while only a little produces a golden tone. A white horse has no pigment at all in its hair. The horse color genes work by determining which pigment will be present in the hairs, what shape the droplets will take, and how dense the droplets will be in the hairs.

The pigment is also found in the skin. In general, dark skin is tougher than light skin and will hold up to the hot sun better than light skin. White markings on a dark horse have pink skin under them, and a truly white horse has pink skin all over its body.

Dappling

Dappling is a pleasing unevenness in the coat color. Light areas of the coat are surrounded by a network of darker areas. The light and dark hairs differ in a basic way. While dappling is most obvious on gray horses, it can occur with any color, even black.

Dappling

A dappled gray

The Basic Colors

You have probably noticed that many horses have black manes, tails, and legs while their bodies are different shades. The mane, tail, and legs are called the *points*. If a horse has a dark brown body and black points, it is called a brown horse. To horsemen, a brown horse always has black points. A horse with black points and red body is called a bay. Bays can be so dark that they look almost black from a distance or they can be very light.

Both these horses look similar in color. However, most horsemen would call the one on the left, which has more light areas, a bay. The other horse is brown.

Top: *A bright bay.* Bottom: *A darker bay.*

A reddish horse with points the same color as the body or slightly lighter is called a chestnut. Like bays, chestnuts can be just about any shade of red, from very dark to very light. A dark chestnut, called a liver chestnut, may look black from a distance. The Arabs said of the liver chestnut, "When he flies under the sun, he is the wind."

The horse to the left is a bay. Her brother, standing next to her, is chestnut.

The darker shade of chestnut is called liver chestnut.

One problem with naming horse colors is that not everyone agrees on the names for some colors. Breeders of Thoroughbreds and Arabian horses call all reddish horses chestnuts. But in American Quarter Horse circles, a light red horse is called a sorrel, while a dark red one is a chestnut.

This bright red horse would be called either a chestnut or a sorrel, depending on who was describing it.

A buckskin mare and foal

Chapter Two

Two-tone Horses

Bays and browns aren't the only horses with manes and tails differently colored from their bodies. Other horses, too, may have darker manes, tails, and legs, and some have lighter manes and tails.

Buckskins and Duns

A buckskin is a striking horse, with a tan or golden body and coal-black points. A buckskin may also sport a neat black stripe along the back from the mane all the way to the tail. Some also have "zebra stripes"—black stripes across the upper legs.

Like a buckskin, a *grulla* (pronounced GREW-ya) has black points. But its body is blue-gray instead of golden or tan. Some grullas look very blue, while others, especially after being out in the sun, have a yellowish tone.

 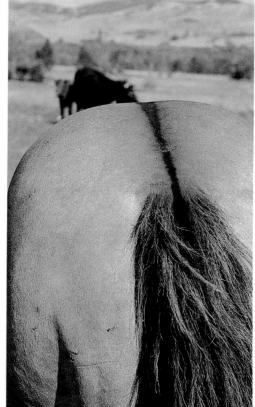

Left: Zebra stripes. Right: The line on the back of a grulla.

A red dun is like a buckskin, except that it has a yellowish body and dark red points, as well as a red stripe down its back.

Both grullas and buckskins are actually also types of duns. Unfortunately, the term dun is used to mean different things. Some people reserve the word dun for a light horse with black points and a stripe down the back. Others call all horses with light yellowish bodies duns, whether or not they have dark points. This use of the word makes some sense, since all duns result from the presence of a *dilution gene*. The different sorts of duns are the result of diluting, or lightening, the color of blacks, bays, and chestnuts. The grulla is a diluted black, while the buckskin is a diluted bay. A dun without dark points results from one kind of dilution of chestnut. Duns are most common among Quarter Horses and mustangs. There are no Arabian or Thoroughbred duns.

A red dun

Lighter Manes and Tails

Often, a chestnut horse will have a cream-colored or white mane and tail. In some breeds, such as the American Belgian, a strong workhorse, this color combination is very common. Breeders of American Belgians use the word sorrel to describe these beautiful horses when their bodies are light red. Some other people, too, are more likely to call a horse sorrel if it has a lighter mane and tail.

These American Belgians have cream-colored manes and tails.

For many, the ultimately beautiful horse is the golden palomino, with its gleaming yellow coat and its white mane and tail. In old Spain, the palomino was honored by giving it the name of the queen, Isabella. Some say that the American name, palomino, came from the golden California grape of the same name. The ancestors of the American palomino came over with the early Spanish explorers, and the palomino color is especially common now in Mexico and California, where the Spanish influence is strongest.

The palomino is actually a chestnut horse that carries a gene which dilutes out the red color, resulting in the pleasing golden tones. Some palominos have dark skin, while others have light hides.

Two Palominos graze together.

A dark brown horse that looks almost black

Chapter Three

White Horse / Black Horse

It should be easy to tell when a horse is white and when it is black. But these opposites may actually be the trickiest to identify. You might look out onto a field and see several horses together, all of which look black. If you looked closely, you might find that each was actually a different color! When you got near one of those "black" horses, you might notice that there are tan areas around its muzzle or just in front of its hind legs. The horse isn't black at all—it is a brown. If there is tan not only in those areas but also on the upper legs or on its shoulders, you have found yourself a dark bay.

A true black horse is black over its entire body. It may have white on its legs or face, but the rest of its body is a uniform black. During the summer, some black horses are bleached by the sun so that they take on a reddish tone.

A true black Quarter Horse stallion.

This black wild horse has a faded mane from being out in the summer sun.

Between Black and White

One other problem can confuse the question of the black horse. Many horses that are born black turn gray as they grow older. This is especially common in some breeds, such as the heavy Percheron. Almost all Percherons are born black, but a few telltale gray hairs will be present in those that are destined to become gray.

Gray horses become more and more gray as they age. When you see a horse that looks white, chances are it really isn't white. It is more likely to be an older gray. The famous performing Lippizaner horses are all born black or dark brown. As they grow older, they get more and more white hairs until they appear snow white. Many gray Arabian horses also become very white. Grays that have turned white have black skin and dark eyes. If you look at the face of one of these horses, you can easily see the black skin on the muzzle.

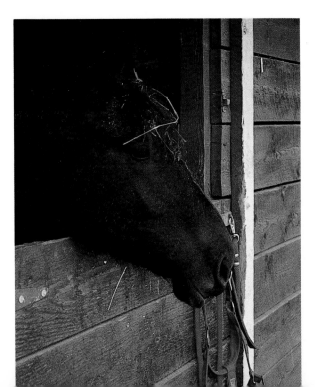

The telltale white hairs on this Percheron show that it will turn gray with time.

Top: These two "white" Percherons are actually older grays. Notice the few black hairs on their faces. Bottom: This Percheron mare is actually an older gray. Her foal will either remain black or gradually turn white, like its mother.

All four of these gray Percherons will eventually be white.

Variations on Gray

Any color horse can be born with the gene that makes it become more and more white with age. Most breeds refer to all such horses as grays. For this reason, gray horses can have different color patterns. If the colored hairs on the coat are black, the horse will appear gray. If the hairs are red, however, the horse will look pinkish. Some people call this color rose gray. The mane and tail of a gray may stay dark, or they may turn white when or before most of the body does. Some older grays develop flecks of reddish hair all over their bodies. They are called "flea-bitten" grays.

Top: This rose gray Arabian is quite light in color. Bottom: A
flea-bitten gray Arabian mare. Notice the black skin on her muzzle.

Cremellos and Perlinos

There are still other kinds of "white" horses that aren't really white. While the palomino results from a dilution of chestnut, a double dilution of chestnut produces an even paler horse called the *cremello*. A cremello has blue eyes and hair that is very close to white. A double dilution of bay results in another close-to-white horse called a *perlino*. The points of a cremello are the same color as the body, while those of a perlino are darker.

This perlino is very close to white, but if you look closely, you can see that it is not.

The Truly White Horse

In many kinds of animals, white individuals with no melanin at all in their hair or skin may be born. These are called *albinos*. Albinos have white hair and pink eyes. In horses, however, there are no true albinos. White horses with blue, brown, or hazel eyes are born, but never ones with pink eyes.

It is hard to keep a white horse clean. This one is snowy white when all washed and brushed for a show.

Roan Horses

Roan is another pattern in which white hairs are mixed with other colors. Roans usually look quite different from grays, however. While grays often turn white first on their heads, roans generally have dark heads. Once a roan has lost its foal coat, it shows the color it will be the rest of its life. Unlike a gray, it doesn't get lighter with time.

Like gray, roan can appear in combinations with any other coat color. Roan on black, brown, or very dark bay looks blue, so it is called blue roan. Bay roans are called red

A red roan foal grazes next to its blue roan mother.

A blue roan

roan, while roan on sorrel is called strawberry roan. A strawberry roan with a very dark mane and tail is hard to tell from a red roan.

Unfortunately, roan gets us into name problems again. Roan does not appear in Thoroughbred horses, but gray does. To distinguish a red gray from a black and white one that looks gray to the eye, the Thoroughbred breeders call a red gray a roan. If you keep track of horse racing and see a horse referred to as a roan, you will know that it is really a red gray and will become lighter with age, just like any other gray.

A foal with a star

Chapter Four

Blazes and Socks

Many horses have striking white markings on their faces and legs that accent their lovely colors. Because it may be important to be able to describe or identify an individual horse, each type of marking has a specific name.

Stars and Stripes

A white marking on a horse's face can accent its beauty or give it a strange look. A star is a white mark between the eyes; it can be any shape. The Arabs valued especially a black horse with a white star, "which shines like the first glow of dawn." A narrow band of white in the area between the forehead and the nostrils is called a strip, while a bit of white on the nose is called a snip. A blaze is a broad stripe of white that extends the entire length of the face. If the blaze is very wide and covers part of the eyes and nostrils, it is called a

A star can be just a tiny spot of white.

A wide blaze

This mare has a star and strip. Her foal has a star, strip, and snip.

bald face. An apron face has white that covers the entire lower part of the head, including the lower lips.

Often a horse will have a combination of face markings, and they are sometimes connected. Both markings are then mentioned—"star and strip," "star and snip," and so forth. Instead of the terms strip and blaze, Thoroughbred breeders use one word, stripe, for a marking that begins at eye level or below and ends on or above the upper lip.

A star and strip that are joined.

White Leg Markings

Since a horse has four legs and each can have no white, a bit of white, or lots of it, leg markings are especially useful in identifying individual animals. A white band that runs just around the top of the hoof is called a coronet. If the white extends partway up onto what looks like the ankle of the horse, called the pastern, the marking is called a half pastern. If it covers the entire pastern joint, it is simply called a pastern.

The left front foot of this horse has a coronet.

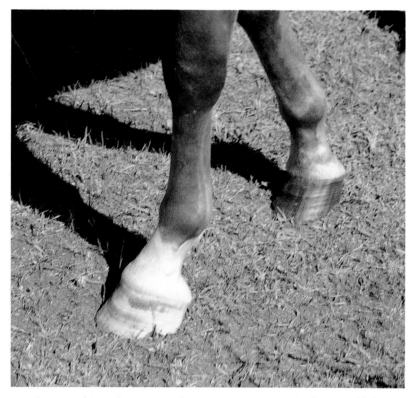

A white marking that covers the entire pastern of the leg is called a pastern. Note that the hoof below the white marking is light, while the other hoof is black.

Markings that extend partway up to the knee joint on a front leg or to the back-leg joint, the hock, are called socks. Stockings, on the other hand, go all the way up to the joint.

A dark horse with four white socks or stockings looks very flashy while trotting. All horses chosen to be Budweiser Clydesdales have four white stockings so that their high-stepping gait is accented.

This foal with four socks will be a flashy runner.

Good and Bad Marks

The Arabs had prejudices about white on the faces and legs of their horses. If a black horse had a star and three white legs, but not a white right foreleg, it was considered especially beautiful. But four white legs made the horse just about worthless to them! While the star was valued, a horse with a stripe that didn't reach the upper lip, along with a white foreleg, meant very bad luck.

The Arabs also avoided horses with bald faces. There are good reasons for that, because when white extends over the eyes, the eyes are often lighter in color and more sensitive to the sun. The white hair and pink skin around the eyes can reflect too much light as well, resulting in eye strain for the animal on bright, sunny days, even if its eyes are dark.

The hooves below white markings also often lack pigment. Many horsemen think that dark hooves are stronger than light ones. In some horses, especially Appaloosas, the hooves may be vertically striped.

This horse has socks on its hind legs and stockings on its forelegs. When white extends all the way around the front of the face like this, it is called an "apron face."

Striped hooves

A tobiano

Chapter Five

Spots and Patches

While many people love a bay, chestnut, or gray horse, others prefer something flashier. They want a horse with a pattern that will make heads turn. Such folks are the lovers of spotted horses—paints, with their big splashes of white, and Appaloosas, with their patterns of smaller spots.

Pintos and Paints

A friend once said, "I can't seem to keep straight the differences between pintos and paints." No wonder—there is no difference! Pinto and paint are simply words used to describe horses with patches of white on a different base color such as black or bay.

Some people think of paints mostly as Indian ponies. They picture warriors galloping across the plains on their colorful mounts. The Plains Indians did appreciate the paint's colorful coat, but the paint pattern is found in horses around the world. There are actually two kinds of paints, the *overo* and the *tobiano*. The tobiano is the most common in the United States. The white patches usually have definite edges to them, and some white almost always crosses over the back. The legs of a tobiano are usually white. The face may have markings, but not the extensive white associated with the overo.

A tobiano

A typical overo

The overo has patches of white with a more irregular outline. The white rarely crosses the back, and one or more legs may be solid colored. In contrast to the tobiano, the overo usually has a great deal of white on its head, usually giving it a bald face.

Either spotting pattern can occur over any of the basic colors. The British have special terms to describe paints. A piebald horse is black with white spots, while a skewbald horse is a paint with no black. The paint patterns on bay results in a three-color horse—white, red, and black. These animals are especially striking when the white patches include parts of the mane and tail.

Both patterns can also be very limited or very extensive. Some tobianos have only white legs and a patch or two on the body, while an overo may have only a bald face and a couple of small spots.

A piebald tobiano

Appaloosa Patterns

The Appaloosa horse is the colorful result of breeding by the Nez Percé tribe of Indians that lived in what is now southeastern Washington and nearby areas. These Indians wanted fast, tough horses, and the spotted patterns appealed to them. The color patterns that are associated in American minds with this breed actually occur in many horses around the world, too, including the Pony of the Americas, the Colorado Ranger, the Knabstrup of Denmark, and various kinds of wild and Indian horses.

Perhaps the most familiar Appaloosa pattern is the blanket. The body of the horse can be any base color, but there is a patch of white over the horse's rump, often with spots or flecks of color. The blanket can vary in size from a

An Appaloosa with a blanket.

small area of white to one that reaches all the way to the front legs and covers part of the belly.

The leopard pattern is especially striking. The horse is white and is marked with spots. The pattern of the spots often makes it looks as if they flow from the sides of the horse. While most leopard-patterned horses have dark spots, the pattern can also occur with light-colored spots.

Instead of having a white body with dark spots, some

A leopard Appaloosa

Appaloosas have a dark body with white spots; this is called the snowflake pattern. Other Appaloosas have a roan coat different from the standard roan. There are white hairs on the head, and the colored hairs are more dense where the bones come close to the skin—the shoulders, knees, hips, and so forth. In Appaloosa circles, this is called a varnish roan.

Appaloosas are also known for their mottled look, especially around the face and under the belly. White hair is randomly mixed in with the base color, and where the hair is thin, such as on the nose and around the eyes, there is a mixture of pink and dark skin. The mottling can also extend onto other parts of the horse, giving it a frosted look.

A varnish roan Appaloosa

This Appaloosa mare has a mottled coat with an overlying snowflake pattern. Her foal has a blanket.

Mixed-up Patterns

Sometimes, so many different pattern genes are affecting the color of a horse that it is hard to separate them all and describe the color in a reasonable way. Among wild horses, whose breeding is not controlled by humans, and rodeo stock, which are not bred for color but for their ability to buck, strange combinations of colors can turn up. While scientists understand how the basic horse colors are inherited, they still do not know exactly how many of the flashier patterns, such as the overo and the blanket, are determined.

There is much more to learn about horse color, and many confusions about names to be cleared up. But while other people struggle with these problems, the rest of us can relax and enjoy the colorful variety of that special animal, the horse.

Wild horses can show a variety of colors.

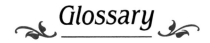 Glossary

Apron-face horse—a horse with a wide band of white on its face that covers the entire lower part of the head, including the lower lips.

Bald-face horse—a horse with a wide white blaze on its face that covers part of the eyes and nostrils.

Bay horse—a horse with a red coat and black points.

Blanket—a pattern in which the horse's rump is white, often with black spots, while the rest of the body is a different color.

Blaze—a wide stripe of white that extends the entire length of a horse's face.

Brown horse—a horse with a brown coat and black points.

Buckskin—a horse with a tan or yellowish coat and black points.

Chestnut horse—a horse with a red coat. The points are either the same color or lighter.

Coronet—a white marking that forms a narrow band just above a horse's hoof.

Cremello—an almost white horse with points the same color.

Dappling—a pattern in which light areas of the coat are surrounded by a network of darker areas.

Dun—a lighter coat color which results from the dilution of a darker color. The word is not used in the same way by everyone.

Eumelanin—a brown or black pigment found in horses.

Gray horse—a horse with white hairs mixed with another color. A gray becomes more and more white with age and often ends up completely white.

Grulla—a blue-gray horse with black points.

Half pastern—a white marking that extends partway up the "ankle" of a horse's leg.

Leopard—a pattern of variably sized black or brown spots on a white horse.

Liver chestnut—a very dark chestnut horse.

Melanin—a dark pigment.

Mottling—a mixing of white and darker hairs, with underlying pink and dark skin, on a horse. Mottling is most often noticed on the faces of Appaloosa horses.

Overo—a paint horse with irregular-looking patches. White rarely crosses the animal's back, and one or more legs may be solid colored.

Paint—a horse with patches of white and dark hair.

Palomino—a golden horse with a white mane and tail.

Pastern—a white marking that covers the entire "ankle" of a horse's leg.

Perlino—an almost white horse with darker points.

Phaeomelanin—a reddish pigment found in horses.

Piebald—a British term for a black-and-white paint horse.

Pinto—the same as a paint.

Pigment—a colored substance such as melanin.

Points—the mane, tail, and lower legs of a horse.

Red dun—a light red horse with dark red points.

Roan—a horse with white hairs mixed in with dark ones. After losing its foal coat, a roan stays the same color all its life.

Rose gray—a horse with red and white hairs on its body, which gives it a pinkish tone. A rose gray turns more white with age.

Skewbald—a British term for a nonblack paint.

Snip—a bit of white between the nostrils of a horse's face.

Snowflake—a pattern of white spots on a darker background.

Sock—a white marking that extends partway to the knee joint of a horse's leg.

Sorrel—one term for a light red horse, often used when the mane and tail are lighter than the body.

Star—a white mark between a horse's eyes.

Stocking—a white marking that extends all the way to the knee of a horse's leg.

Strip—a narrow band of white that runs between the forehead and nostrils of a horse.

Tobiano—a paint horse with dark patches with definite edges. Almost always, some white crosses the animal's back, and its legs are usually white.

Index

636.1   Patent, Dorothy
PAT   Hinshaw.

A horse of a
different color

$13.95   1755

DATE			